THE FLOWERS OF BUFFOONERY

THE FLOWERS
OF BUFFOONERY

BY OSAMU DAZAI

TRANSLATED BY SAM BETT

A NEW DIRECTIONS PAPERBOOK

First published as New Directions Paperbook 1552 in 2023
Manufactured in the United States of America

Library of Congress Cataloging-in-Publication Data
Names: Dazai, Osamu, 1909–1948, author. | Bett, Sam, 1986– translator.
Title: The flowers of buffoonery / by Osamu Dazai ; translated by Sam Bett.
Other titles: Dōke no hana. English
Description: First edition. | New York : New Directions Books, 2023. |
"A New Directions paperbook" |
Identifiers: LCCN 2022050259 | ISBN 9780811234542 (paperback) |
ISBN 9780811234559 (ebook)
Subjects: LCGFT: Novels.
Classification: LCC PL825.A8 D6513 2023 | DDC 895.63/44—dc23/eng/20221017
LC record available at https://lccn.loc.gov/2022050259

10 9 8 7 6

New Directions Books are published for James Laughlin
by New Directions Publishing Corporation
80 Eighth Avenue, New York 10011

THE FLOWERS OF BUFFOONERY

"Welcome to Sadness. Population one."

All my friends have left me. They look back at me with eyes of pity. Come back, friends. Let's talk together, laugh together. But no, you turn away as if we've never met. Speak up, friends. Ask away. I'll tell you anything. It was me – these are the hands that pulled Sono underwater. In my satanic insolence, I prayed for my salvation in the same breath that I prayed Sono would die.

Shall I go on? But why bother, friends, if you'll only look at me with pity in your eyes?

Yozo Oba sat on the bed, staring at the sea. A sea clouded with rain.

As if waking from a dream, I reread these first few

lines and want to disappear into their ugliness and obscenity. But there I go again with my ridiculous exaggerations.

To begin, who is this Yozo Oba character? I wrote him into being, drunk on a substance far more potent than alcohol. There could be no better name for my protagonist. "Oba" flawlessly encapsulates his vigorous spirit, while "Yozo," I must say, has pizazz. It conveys a certain freshness, to be accessed only if one sinks into the depths of the old-fashioned. Not to mention the phonic harmony of those four vowel sounds in a row. Yozo Oba. Have I not already dazzled you with my creations? Well then, feast your eyes on Yozo Oba, our protagonist, seated on the bed and staring at a sea clouded with rain. As dazzling a creation as they come!

Enough. Shame on me for making such a mockery of myself. Blame it on my wounded pride. The fact is that my fear of being ridiculed is so intense I'd rather beat my critics to the punch. That's the epitome of cowardice. I must find a way to be more modest. Ah, humility.

Yozo Oba.

Go ahead and laugh. He is a crow dressed as a cormorant. The perceptive will perceive what I am up to. Sure, I could've come up with a better name, but I guess I can't be bothered. I might have skirted the whole issue by writing this in the first person, but this past spring I wrote a novel with a first-person narrator, so I'm hesitant to do another one so soon. Besides, if I were to drop dead tomorrow, we can't be sure some smart aleck wouldn't set forth the sage opinion that without a first-person narrator, the novel never would have worked. And if I'm honest, this is my only reason for letting Yozo Oba survive, as you find him here. You think that's odd? Well, right back at you, friend.

ろ

In 1929, toward the end of December, a seaside sanatorium by the name of Blue Pines Manor lit up with the arrival of one Yozo Oba. Blue Pines had thirty-six tuberculosis patients. Two in critical condition, eleven mild cases, and another twenty-three who were in remission. The Eastern Wing, where Yozo would be staying, consisted of a hallway with six rooms, side by side, where the "special cases" were accommodated. The rooms on either side of him were vacant, while Room 1, the first room in the hall, was occupied by a tall college student with a Roman nose. Sleeping in Rooms 5 and 6, on the far end, were a pair of young women. All three of these patients were in recovery.

10

The previous night, there had been a lover's suicide at Tamotogaura, a cliff just down the shore. A couple had thrown themselves into the sea, but the man had been picked up by a fishing boat sailing into port, which saved his life. The woman's body, however, was nowhere to be found. Firefighters formed a search party and hammered on the fire bell for what seemed like an eternity and yelled "Heave-Ho!" into the night, launching every last fishing boat at their disposal.

The three patients in the Eastern Wing listened to the sounds over the pounding of their hearts. All night long the brilliant torches on the fishing boats swept the cliffside of the tidal island of Enoshima. Neither the college student nor the two young girls were able to sleep. At dawn, the woman's body washed up on the beach at Tamotogaura. Her short-cropped hair was lustrous, her face swollen and pale.

Yozo knew Sono was dead. He knew it from the moment that the fishing boat had picked him from the choppy waves. When he came to, under the starlight, the first thing that he asked was, "Is she dead?" But a fisherman assured him, in a voice thick with benevolence, "She ain't dead, she ain't dead. No need to worry."

So she is dead, he told himself, but soon lost consciousness.

The next time he opened his eyes, he was in the sanatorium. A cramped room clad in whitewashed boards. The room was full of people. Somebody was asking him all kinds of things about himself. He answered all the questions plainly.

At daybreak, he was transferred to a different room, this one more spacious. His family had telephoned Blue Pines long distance to check up on him as soon as they got word of the event. They lived almost five hundred miles away.

The three patients of the Eastern Wing were inordinately pleased to welcome this new patient as a neighbor. Such was their excitement that they only fell asleep after the sky and sea had both transitioned fully into day.

Yozo lay awake, turning his head gently from time to time. Face partly hidden in white gauze. Body bruised from being eaten by the waves and dashed against the rocks. A nurse by the name of Mano, around twenty, was entrusted with his care. A rather large scar over her left eyelid made her left eye look a little bigger than the right. But she was not unsightly. Her cherry-colored upper lip curled up ever so slightly and her cheeks were a healthy tan. From her seat by Yozo's bed, she watched the ocean underneath the cloudy sky, doing her best not to look at Yozo's face. He was so pitiful she couldn't bear it.

Around noon, two detectives paid Yozo a visit. Mano left the room.

The men were genteel, dressed in suits. One had a short mustache, the other steel-framed glasses. Mustache lowered his voice and asked how he and Sono had become acquainted with each other. Yozo told him everything there was to tell. Mustache took notes on a little memo pad. Once he was finished with his first round of questions, Mustache leaned over the bed and said, "She's dead, you know. And I'm not so sure you were prepared to join her."

Yozo was silent.

Steel-Framed Glasses smiled, so that a few impressive wrinkles gathered on his fleshy brow, and clapped his mustachioed partner on the shoulder. "All right, all right. He's tired. It can wait."

Without taking his eyes off Yozo for an instant, Mustache begrudgingly returned the memo pad to the pocket of his jacket.

As soon as the detectives made their leave, Mano came rushing back into the room, only to find Yozo in tears. Without a second thought, she gently closed the door and waited in the hall.

It rained that afternoon. Yozo had recovered enough strength to be able to stand up and walk over to the lavatory on his own.

His friend Hida waltzed into the room wearing a damp overcoat. Yozo pretended to be asleep.

"Is he okay?" Hida asked Mano in a whisper.

"Sure, he's fine."

"Quite the scare."

Contorting his chubby arms, he doffed the rank oil-skin and handed it to Mano.

Hida was a no-name sculptor. His friendship with Yozo, himself an unknown painter, extended back to middle school. At that tender age, it's natural for the pure of heart among us to look up to someone in our social circle as a kind of idol, which is precisely what he did with Yozo. Since the start of middle school, Hida had gazed with admiration at the best students in his class, but Yozo was the best of the best. His every frown or smile was, to Hida, ripe with meaning. The time he spotted Yozo all alone on the hill behind the school, he let out a deep sigh, making sure nobody noticed. But what could top the joy of the first day they conversed? From then on, Hida openly copied everything that Yozo did. He smoked cigarettes. Sneered at his teachers. Made a practice of pacing the schoolyard with both hands clasped pensively behind his head. And of course he learned why artists are superior to all. Yozo went off to art school; and though Hida graduated a year after him, he managed to get into the same program. Yozo majored in painting, but Hida deliberately switched over to sculpture. He liked to say he owed it all to Rodin's *Monument to Balzac*, but this was just a bit of nonsense he tacked onto his personal mythology, something to casually refer to once he had become a maestro, when in reality he was intimidated by Yozo's talent as a painter.

This was the point when their paths finally diverged. Yozo was getting skinnier all the time, while Hida made up for the difference, packing on the pounds. But this was not the only thing setting them apart. Yozo was lured in by a certain brand of populist philosophy and became critical of fine art.

Hida, meanwhile, got a little too high on his own work, spouting so much art world gibberish that anyone who heard him talk was embarrassed on his behalf. Fantasies about creating an indisputable masterpiece distracted him from school.

Both of them graduated with low marks. Yozo had all but tossed aside the paintbrush.

"A painting is just a glorified poster," he told Hida, putting him in his place. "Art is a proverbial turd, the byproduct of the socioeconomic complex. Social capital made manifest. Even the greatest masterpiece is no more than a commodity, just like a pair of socks."

These vague generalizations left Hida in the dark. He was affectionate as ever to his dear friend Yozo, even mildly impressed with his deployment of contemporary thought, but for Hida the lure of the masterpiece eclipsed all others. Almost there, he told himself, almost there, though he was doing little more than poking at a block of clay.

One might say that these two friends were not actually artists, so much as works of art. Indeed, how else could I have depicted them using such easy brushstrokes? Trust me, dear reader, if I were to present you with a real-life artist, you would puke before you made it through but three lines of description, guaranteed. If you don't believe me, why not try writing a novelistic portrait of an artist for yourself?

Hida had a hard time looking at Yozo's face as well. Tiptoeing like a cat burglar, he plodded his way over to the bedside, where he gazed upon the streaks of rain outside the glass windows.

Yozo opened his eyes and greeted Hida with a smirk. "Gotcha."

Startled, Hida snuck a look at Yozo but immediately averted his eyes.

"Sure did."

"Where'd you hear?"

Hida faltered. Drawing a hand from his trouser pocket, he wiped his palm across his face and cast a furtive glance at Mano, as if to ask if it was safe to tell him. Mano's expression was severe; she shook her head ever so slightly.

"Was it in the papers?"

"That's right."

In fact, Hida had heard it on the news, over the radio.

Yozo was repelled by Hida's milquetoast bearing. Loosen up already, will you? He had awoken to a world turned upside down, in which his friend of over ten years held him at arm's length, like he was some kind of an alien.

No thanks. Once again, Yozo pretended to fall asleep.

Hida was jittery. After shuffling around the room for a few minutes in the floppy slippers provided by the hospital, however, he eventually returned to Yozo's bedside.

As the door opened without a sound, a college kid in his school uniform stuck his handsome face into the doorway. At the sight of him, Hida practically moaned with relief. He fended off a smile with a tightness of the cheek and headed for the door at an affectedly slow pace.

"Just get in?" asked Hida.

Careful not to look at Yozo, the new guest cleared his throat.

"Yep," he said.

Kosuge was a relative of Yozo. Studying law at university. Though he was three years younger, he dispensed with formalities and met Yozo on his level, as a friend. Youngsters these days appear not to be much concerned with differences in age. He had been home for winter break, but when he heard about what happened to Yozo, he caught the first express train down to the coast.

He and Hida stepped into the hall to talk.

"Your face is covered in soot!" Hida said.

He let out a big belly laugh and pointed at Kosuge's upper lip. Smoke from the locomotive had left a layer of grime on his skin.

"Really?" Kosuge pulled a handkerchief from his chest pocket. He wiped the space under his nose. "Well? How are things shaping out?"

"Oba? Fine, overall."

"Really? Fell, huh." Kosuge made his lip taut, so that Hida could inspect it.

"Yeah, he fell all right. Family must be all worked up."

Kosuge stuffed the handkerchief into his pocket. "They're worked up all right. May as well have been a funeral."

"Is someone coming from the house?"

"His brother is. His father told him not to bother, though."

"What a mess," muttered Hida, hand pressed against his brow.

"Is Yo-Yo really okay?"

"You know him. Happy as a clam."

Kosuge shook his head and smiled, practically elated. "But I wonder how he's really feeling."

"Why not ask him yourself?"

"That's okay. Nothing to say. And besides – he's a mess."

The two friends snickered.

Mano stepped out into the hall.

"We can hear you in there. Please find somewhere else to talk."

"Ah, sorry."

Embarrassed, Hida made his massive body as small as possible. Kosuge gave Mano a curious look.

"Have the two of you, um, eaten lunch?" she asked.

"Not yet," they said in unison.

Mano blushed and burst out laughing at their timing.

As the three of them were just about to set off for the cafeteria, Yozo sat up. Once again, he was staring at the sea clouded with rain.

"Welcome to Darkness. Population none."

Which brings us back to the beginning. A bit clumsily, if I do say so myself. I must say, I dislike these narrative contrivances. And yet I try to use them nonetheless. Welcome to Sadness. Population one. A poetic line with a familiar ring, straight from the gates of the inferno, but I had thought it might work well here, as a glowing opener. I have no other defense. Even if this one line spelled the downfall of my novel, I'm afraid I wouldn't have the guts to cut it. I might even put it this way, for good measure: deleting that first line would mean erasing my entire life thus far.

は

"I blame that newfangled philosophy. Marxism."

A fabulously silly line of dialogue. Superb.

Kosuge was the one who said it. With a look of satisfaction in his eyes, he reached once more for his cup of milk.

All four walls of the wood-paneled cafeteria were painted white. High on the eastern wall there hung a portrait of the director wearing three smart medals shaped like copper coins, under the gaze of which ten or so tables stood modestly on spindly legs. The cafeteria was dead. Hida and Kosuge were seated in the southeast corner, having lunch.

"He was really pushing himself hard," Kosuge said,

lowering his voice. "Running all over the place with that frail body of his. No wonder he wanted to die."

"You realize he's the captain of his local chapter of the party." Hida munched away on a piece of bread, taking big bites. He wasn't showing off his knowledge of communist shorthand. Any young man of his generation was familiar with the jargon of the left. "But there's something else going on here. Artists never do things just to do them, you know."

The cafeteria went dark. The rain was getting stronger.

Kosuge took another sip of milk. "There you go again, taking things personally. Here's the thing, though. Behind any given suicide, there's always going to be some external factor, something too big for the person who goes through with it to see. The whole family is convinced the woman is to blame, but I told them, look, that can't be the entire story. She was just roped into things. There's got to be some other, larger explanation. They don't get it. And now you're talking nonsense, too. Wise up."

Hida stared into the flames of a stove burning by their feet. "But the woman, she was married, right?"

Kosuge set down his cup of milk.

"I know. What of it? I doubt it even crossed his mind. Come on, dying with your lover just because she has a husband? Give me a break." He craned his neck to get a look at the portrait hung above them. "Is this the guy in charge?"

"Guess so. But look – Oba is the only one who really knows what happened."

"Sure," Kosuge said, agreeing noncommittally, then looked around the room. "Kind of a draft in here. You gonna spend the night?"

Hida wolfed down another piece of bread and nodded. "Yup."

These boys never really argue. Ever so careful with each other's feelings, they tiptoe from one comment to the next, taking great pains to shelter their own feelings in the process. They'll do anything to avoid being ridiculed. Truly, they're convinced that if they ever did do something hurtful, they'd either have to kill the other guy or die themselves. It's why they avoid conflict as a rule. These friends know all kinds of expressions that could smooth things over. At least ten different gradations for conveying what essentially means "no." Long before any type of conflict can emerge, they're exchanging gestures of diplomacy. And while they dance across the surface with their smiles and their handshakes, in their minds they're both saying the same thing: what an idiot!

Well then, my novel has at last begun to lose its marbles. For a change of pace, how about a few panoramic vignettes? Not to get your hopes up. Clumsy good-for-nothing fool that I am. All right, here goes nothing.

The next morning was peaceful and clear. The sea was calm. White smoke from the volcano on Oshima, just above the horizon, drifted up into the sky.

Never mind. I hate describing scenery.

The patient in Room 6 opened her eyes to find the room was flooded with the light of early spring. She exchanged good mornings with her nurse, who promptly took her temperature. It was 97.5°F. With that out of the way, they went out onto the balcony for some sunbathing before mealtime. She didn't need the nurse's gentle prod to notice that the new patient was sunning on his balcony as well, seated in a rattan chair a few rooms down. He wore a lined kimono, blue with white dots, neatly

25

tied. He was staring at the sea, squinting his bushy eyebrows in the glare. Not exactly a handsome face, so far as she could see. At intervals, he tapped the back of his hand on the gauze wound around his cheeks.

Reclined on a daybed made for sunbathing, she watched her neighbor for a while, as her eyes adjusted to the day, before asking her nurse for a book. *Madame Bovary*, to be specific. So far the novel was a bore, tough to get through five or six pages without tossing it aside, but today she was determined to make progress. Reading this book at this particular moment seemed all too appropriate to her. She flipped ahead and jumped in around page 100, where she picked up a great line: "A midnight wedding, lit with torches, is what Emma really wanted."

The patient in Room 5 was awake now, too. Stepping out onto the balcony to enjoy the sun, she saw Yozo down the way and scrambled back into her room. It spooked her so much that she climbed back into bed. Her mother, who was looking after her, laughed as she covered her up with a blanket. The patient pulled the blanket over her head and flashed her eyes in the private darkness, listening to the voice coming from next door.

"She's a looker!" it said, followed by a sneaky laugh.

Hida and Kosuge had spent the night in Room 4, sharing a bed. Kosuge woke first and appeared outside on the balcony, squinting at the light. From the corner of his eye he glanced at Yozo, who was reclined in an affected pose, then followed his friend's line of sight to discover what had caused him to put on this little show. A young woman on the very last balcony was reading a book. Behind her daybed was a stone wall covered with damp moss. Kosuge shrugged his shoulders like they did in Hollywood movies and ducked inside to rouse Hida from his slumber.

"Get up. We've got a situation on our hands." These boys enjoyed creating situations. "Yo-Yo's doing a major pose."

In their conversations, "major" was frequently employed as an intensifying adjective. This world can be a boring place. Who can blame them for wanting something exciting to happen?

"What now?"

Hida, frightened, sat straight up.

Kosuge smiled and explained.

"There's a girl out there. Yo-Yo's giving her his signature profile."

Hida started bouncing on the bed. Both of them sent their eyebrows halfway up their foreheads, trading suggestive looks. "Is she good-looking?"

"She's a looker, all right. Out there pretending to be reading."

Hida burst out laughing. Sitting up in bed, he pulled on his jacket and his pants, then shouted, "All right, let's teach him a lesson."

They intended nothing of the sort. They were pa-lavering. These boys palavered on and on about their friends like it was nothing. They let the spirit move them.

"Oba won't stop till he's had every woman on the planet."

After a time, a round of raucous laughter exploded from Yozo's room, echoing throughout the wing. The patient staying in Room 6 snapped her book shut and looked suspiciously toward Yozo's balcony. But all she found was a white rattan chair, bathed in morning sun, nobody there. Staring at the empty chair, she nodded off.

When the patient in Room 5 heard the laugh, she tossed away the blanket and exchanged cheerful smiles with her mother, who was standing at her bedside.

The laughter woke the college student in Room 1. He had no one assigned to look after him and was free, like a tenant in a boarding house, to do whatever he pleased. Upon realizing the laugh had come from the room of the patient who had arrived the day before, his ashen face turned red. And not because he found the laugh to be indecent. On the contrary, he was awash with human kindness of the sort unique to patients in recovery. It was deeply reassuring to hear such a resounding sign of health coming from Yozo.

Am I a third-rate novelist or what? I can't help feeling like this sounds a bit too precious. I start off promising you something outrageous as a panoramic vignette, but in no time, I've slipped back into my usual complacency.

Wait, though. I have a line prepared to explain away this very failing:

Beautiful feelings make bad literature.

In which case, this precious spate of prose is proof that I'm no devil after all. Ah, blessed be the man who coined this phrase! It is a treasure of the language. An author can get away with using it but once in his career. Sad to say. The first time, it's endearing. If you insist on using it a second or a third time, though, dear reader, hiding behind it like a shield, you can expect nothing but misery.

"I flubbed it!" Kosuge said decisively, seated on the sofa beside Hida.

He looked at Hida's face, then Yozo's face, then Mano, who was leaning against the door, to make sure that all of them were smiling, one by one, before burying his own face, with a look of satisfaction, in the roundness of Hida's right shoulder. These guys were laughing all the time. Cracking up at the dumbest things, completely beside themselves. For these boys, smiling came as naturally as breathing, and laughter easy as an exhalation. It makes you wonder where they picked the habit up. To them, laughing was safe, but not laughing posed a serious risk. They found it irresistible. One might say that they were gluttonous for laughter, unable to pass up even a stray crumb, out of fear they might be questioned for withholding. The sad thing about all of this, however, is that none of them could laugh from the bottom of their bellies. Even as they doubled over laughing, they took notice of the way they looked to one another.

And it should come as no surprise that they loved making other people laugh as well, even if they had to hurt themselves to do so. Another instance of their nihilism, to be sure. But should you scratch below the surface, I think you'll find a personal imperative to serve. Call it a sense of sacrifice. An aimless sense of sacrifice, lacking a clear objective. Any acts of heroism they had managed to achieve, as we define such things in terms of moral law, could be explained away as the byproduct of this latent need to serve.

Well, then. What follows is my personal perspective. And it's not some fantasy dreamt up inside a dusty study. All of it is based on things I heard in person, with my own two ears.

Yozo was still laughing. Seated on the bed, he wobbled both his legs and laughed like crazy, careful not to lose his gauze. Was the story Kosuge had told them all that funny? To illustrate what sort of story cracked these fellows up, let me provide a few choice lines.

During his recent holiday, Kosuge had ventured

to a famous spa town in the mountains, not ten miles from his home, to do some skiing, and stayed over at the lodge. In the middle of the night, he got up to use the bathroom. On his way down the hallway, he passed by a young lady who was staying in the same inn.

That was it. But to him, this was a major situation. All he did was pass her in the hall, but it filled Kosuge with a dire need to be seen by her and impress her with his matchless personality. As foolish as this may have been, he summoned all his energies and, in the instant that they passed each other, struck a pose. Genuinely expecting life to go the way he planned.

In the space of a moment, he considered all the different paths that had brought the two of them together, becoming so emotional that his heart was nearly bursting. These guys had a breathtaking experience like this at least once a day. Hence they were always on the lookout. Even when they were alone, they tried out different poses, constantly refining their appearances.

This might explain why, in the middle of the night, Kosuge was wearing a brand-new blue overcoat on his way down the hall to the bathroom. As soon as she had passed him he felt certain it had been a great success. Good thing he wore his coat! Sighing with relief, he paused at the large mirror at the end of the hallway, to enjoy a moment of reflection, but then he saw that he had flubbed it after all. At the hem of his blue overcoat, his grubby long johns were visible for all to see.

"Man oh man," Kosuge said, having a laugh himself. "My long johns were bunched up at the knees, you know, so you could see my hairy legs. My face puffed up from sleeping."

On the inside, Yozo barely laughed at all. He wouldn't be surprised if Kosuge had made the whole thing up. And yet he laughed out loud, as loudly as the others. His friends were making a good effort to be social with him, unlike yesterday, and in an effort to repay them for their kindness, he cracked up even harder. Hida and Mano got the picture. As long as Yozo was laughing, they laughed too.

This scene made Hida feel most reassured. He knew that it was safe to speak his mind. But he was waiting for the right moment to bring it up. It was hard to tell when that might be.

Kosuge, for his part, was excited now and spoke his mind with ease.

"Our gang has bad luck with the ladies. Even you, Yo-Yo."

Yozo was still laughing, but he shook his head.

"Think so?"

"Yeah. Not worth dying for."

"Sounds like good luck to me."

Hida was beside himself with happiness. Their laughter had knocked down the most treacherous of walls standing between them. This baffling development was due in no small part to Kosuge's endearing brashness. He felt an urge to give his young friend a big bear hug. Raising his thin eyebrows high, he stammered as he spoke.

"Bad luck or not, it's hard to say. Who knows why any of this happened."

Yozo was not pleased with how this sounded, but Kosuge helped him out.

"We do know, though. Hida and I had a major argument about this. I said that it's because our minds can only see so far ahead. Hida, though, he gets really solemn and then tells me there's another angle to consider."

Hida butted in.

"You're right, but only to a point. All I meant was that you must've been in love. Why else would you be willing to die with her?"

Not wanting to give Yozo any room to doubt him, he spoke quickly, without thinking much about his choice of words, but what came out sounded inoffensive to his ears. A major success, he told himself contentedly.

Yozo lowered his eyelashes. All manner of forces swarmed his heart. Haughtiness. Sloth. Flattery. Guile.

Vice. Fatigue. Ferocity. Murder. Despair. Fragility. Deceit. Infection. He came this close to letting them spill out. But instead, he played the role of the heartsick man and groaned.

"To be honest, I don't know myself. Feels like everything's to blame."

"I hear you," said Kosuge, bobbing his head up and down before Yozo could finish. "It happens. Hey, where's your nurse? Guess she's giving us a minute to catch up."

As I started saying earlier, these boys didn't debate to share ideas, so much as to improve whatever mood they happened to be in. Not a word they said was true. But if you tuned in for a moment, there were some unexpected windfalls of veracity. In the middle of a pompous speech, there would sometimes be a phrase of brutal honesty. The things we say without a thought are often how the truth comes out.

Take, for instance, Yozo's way of blaming everything for what had happened. Though said perhaps unconsciously, it revealed his innermost thoughts. Inside the hearts of these young men, you'll find nothing but chaos, that and senseless obstinacy. Or maybe you could sum all of it up as self-importance. And a rarefied self-importance at that. One that shivers and quakes in the slightest breeze. No sooner had they suffered an insult than they wished that they were dead. It was only natural for Yozo to vacillate when asked about the reasoning behind his suicide – it was everything to him.

Early that afternoon, Yozo's older brother arrived at Blue Pines. There was no family resemblance. He was marvelously fat. The pleats of his hakama were pressed.

The director of the sanatorium led him as far as the door to Yozo's room, where they heard a cheerful cry of laughter. Yozo's brother pretended not to recognize the voice.

"It's this one here?" he asked.

"Yes, this is it. He's doing quite well," the director told him, opening the door.

Kosuge, mortified, leapt from the bed. He had been resting there, in Yozo's spot. Yozo and Hida, meanwhile, were seated side by side on the sofa, playing with a deck of cards, but they both scrambled to their feet. Mano was knitting in a chair by the bed, but she too was caught off guard and hurried to stash away her knitting gear.

"His friends have been keeping him company. Keeps the spirits up," the director whispered, looking back toward Yozo's brother as he walked over to the patient's bedside. "You look well, Mr. Oba."

"Thank you," Yozo replied, though doing so made him feel wretched.

The director's eyes were smiling behind his spectacles.

"Life in a sanatorium's not half bad, huh?"

For the first time, Yozo felt the weight of criminality, but he simply responded with a smile.

Meanwhile, his brother was attending to formalities, thanking Hida and Mano for their time and support with a series of stern bows.

He addressed Kosuge separately.

"Did you spend the night here?"

"Yeah," he said, scratching his head. "The room next door was open, so they let me and Hida sleep over."

"Well, tonight you'll be staying with me. I've rented a place on Enoshima. You come along, too, Hida."

"Okay."

Hida froze, unsure of what to do with the three playing cards that he was holding.

The brother turned to Yozo as if everything was settled.

"Yozo, better now?"

"Yeah," he said, making a sour face.

His brother suddenly became a chatterbox.

"Hida, see to it that the director has everything he needs. We're going out for lunch, the whole lot of us. I haven't visited any of the attractions on Enoshima. Perhaps the director would be so kind as to show us around? Let's go. I have a car waiting outside. The weather's fine."

I'm kicking myself for adding these two grownups to the story. They've ruined everything. That titillating atmosphere that I established so adeptly between Yozo, Kosuge, Hida, and myself has fizzled into nothing, thanks to these two adults. I wanted this novel to be an atmospheric romance. Starting with the churning maelstrom of the first few pages. My hope was to tease out and unravel all the different strands. As much as I might call attention to my clumsiness, I somehow got us this far – but now it's all going to pieces.

Forgive me! I made it up. I was playing dumb. I did it all on purpose. As I was writing, I began to feel ashamed of this idea of an, uh, atmospheric romance – so I demolished it intentionally. If things have truly gone to pieces, it was all part of the plan. "Poor taste," you say? Maybe so, but these two words sum up the gnawing feeling in my heart. If poor taste is what you call a perverse interest in intimidating people, it's perhaps a fitting term for how I navigate the world. I'm horrified by failure. I can't bear to have the secrets of my heart revealed. But such efforts are in vain. Ah! Are not all authors the same? So quick to dress up their confessions. I barely qualify as human. Will I ever be a functional member of society? Even as I write these words, I worry how the sentences will sound.

Time to face the facts. This pattern of inserting myself as the narrator between scenes, so that I can burden you with endless rants that no one needs to hear, has an ulterior motive. I've been exploiting my narrative position to hoodwink readers, using this first-person narrator to infuse the work with idiosyncratic nuance. I was arrogant enough to think that I could be the first Japanese author to employ such a sublimely Western style. And yet, I failed. But no, even this confession of failure can be counted as part of the novel's grand design. So you see, I can't be trusted. Don't believe a single word I say.

Why do I bother writing novels? Am I lured by the glory of literary celebrity? Or do I simply want to write bestsellers and cash huge checks? Let me spare you the theatrics. I want both. So bad it hurts. But there I go again, another brazen lie. The sort of lie that ties you up in knots when you're not looking. As despicable and treacherous a lie as they come. Why do I bother writing novels – I had to bring it up. Oh well. At the risk of giving you a pompous explanation, I'll put it this way.

To take revenge.

Let's move on to the next scene. I'm a real-life artist, not a piece of art. If my odious confessions lend this work a modicum of nuance, all the better.

と

Yozo and Mano were left behind. Wide awake, Yozo
climbed into bed and blinked, thinking things over.
Mano sat on the sofa and cleaned up the playing cards.

She slipped the deck into its purple tuck box. "So
that's your older brother?"

"Yeah," said Yozo, eyes fixed on the whitewashed,
lofty ceiling. "Any resemblance?"

Once a writer loses his affection for his subject, his
sentences display a marked decline in quality. Actually,
I take it back. That last one there was snazzy.

"You have the same nose."

Yozo laughed out loud. Everybody in his family had
his grandmother's long nose.

"Must be older, huh?" Mano asked, laughing with him.

"My brother?" Yozo turned her way. "Yeah. He's pretty young, though. Thirty-four. But he walks around like he's a patriarch, all smug and pompous."

Mano snuck a look at Yozo's face. His brow furrowed as he spoke. She hurried to avert her eyes.

"He thinks he's got it all figured out. You see, our father – "

But he stopped himself midsentence. Yozo grew solemn. Working with me, for once, rather than against me. What a sport.

Mano stood up and went over to the shelf in the corner to retrieve her knitting. Same as earlier, she sat down in the chair by Yozo's bed and started to knit, but Mano was thinking too. Not of philosophy, or romance, but one step further, pondering the root cause behind all of this.

I should quit while I'm ahead. The more I say, the less sense I make. It feels like I haven't even scratched the surface of what really matters. And that isn't much of a surprise. I've left out a great deal. Which only makes sense, really. Part of being a novelist is being blind to the value of the work. Painful as it is, I have no choice but to acknowledge this. I am an idiot for thinking that my work would be of consequence to me. And especially for speaking of its consequence as a given. Trying to pin it down with words gave rise to a different set of consequences altogether. And as soon as I began to speculate about these consequences, a new set rushed in to take their place.

I play the role of the fool doomed to chase them down forever. Whether this book is a failure or a fair achievement, it's not for me to say. But if I had to guess, the novel will amount to something of much higher value than I could ever fathom. I came upon this story second-hand. It's not a record of my personal experience. All the more reason that I'm desperate to believe. Frankly, I'm losing faith in my abilities.

ち

The lights came on. Kosuge walked into the room alone and went straight over to Yozo, who was still in bed. He whispered in his ear. Practically smothering him.

"We had a few drinks. Don't tell Mano."

He let out a deep breath in Yozo's face. It was against the rules to return to the hospital if you were drinking.

Glancing back over his shoulder at Mano, who was making progress with her knitting away on the sofa, Kosuge offered a second declaration, loudly this time, for all to hear. "We went sightseeing on Enoshima. It was so much fun." But then he lowered his voice once more to a whisper. "Just kidding."

Yozo got up and sat on the edge of the bed.

"You've been drinking this whole time?" he asked Kosuge. "Not like I care. It's fine. Right, Mano?"

Mano smiled, keeping a steady rhythm with her knitting. "I wouldn't call it fine."

Kosuge lay down on the bed, facing up.

"We had a talk, the bunch of us, you see. With the director. That brother of yours is quite the schemer. Turns out he can really cut a deal."

Yozo was quiet.

"Tomorrow, he and Hida are going down to speak with the police. To make sure everything is on the level. Hida's such an idiot, though. Anxious as hell. He's staying on the island tonight, with your brother. But I was having none of it, so I came back."

"Lemme guess, that brother of mine has been talking behind my back."

"Yup. Called you a jackass. Said there's no telling what trouble you'll get into next. But he said your father isn't any better. Hey, Mano, can I smoke in here?"

"Sure." She was nearly in tears, out of pity for these boys.

"You can hear the waves in here. Not bad for a hospital." Kosuge brought the unlit cigarette to his lips and closed his eyes, panting like a drunkard. A moment later, he sat up straight. "Oh yeah, I brought you a kimono. It's over there."

He gestured toward the doorway with his chin.

Yozo cast his eyes upon the bundle set down by the door, a large furoshiki patterned with karakusa scroll-work. It made him frown. When these young men spoke of their blood relations, their facial expressions became rather sentimental. But it was no more than an act. These expressions were the product of the education they had received from a young age. It would seem that family was no more to them than a euphemism for a bank account.

"Leave it to Mom."

"Yeah, your brother said the same thing. That this whole incident hit her the hardest. She's so concerned. She wanted to make sure you had proper clothes. I feel bad for her, sincerely – Hey, Mano, got a match?" Kosuge took a box of matches from Mano and gazed at the horse face painted on the label. "I gather the director lent you the kimono you have on?"

"This? Yeah. It's his son's, though. What else did my backstabbing brother tell you?"

"Don't get sore now." He touched the struck match to his cigarette. "Your brother's a pretty clued-in guy, I gotta say. He gets you. Well, maybe that's exaggerating. The way he carries himself, though, you'd think he'd seen it all. We had a conversation, all of us, about what was behind, you know, everything that happened to you, but we were laughing the whole time." Kosuge made smoke rings. "As far as he's concerned, you were down and out and needed cash. He really meant it, too. But in a roundabout way, he insinuated that you must have picked up an embarrassing disease and were really desperate."

Kosuge turned to Yozo, bleary-eyed from drinking. "Well? Wouldn't be surprised."

Since Kosuge was the only one spending the night, it seemed like a waste to take up a whole room by himself, so they talked things over and concluded it would be best if he stayed with Yozo. He slept on the sofa beside the bed. Upholstered in green velvet, it had a dubious hinge mechanism that allowed for it to be folded out into a bed. This was normally where Mano slept, but tonight, thanks to Kosuge, she had resorted to sleeping on a mat she borrowed from the office and spread out in the northwest corner of the room, not far from the foot of Yozo's bed. To finish off her accommodations, Mano set up a short folding screen she had scrounged up who knows where, creating a semblance of modesty.

"Not taking any chances, huh?" Nestling into the sofa, Kosuge looked at the ratty screen and giggled. "How about that, it's decorated with the seven flowers of autumn."

Mano wrapped the furoshiki around the bulb dangling over Yozo's head to dim the lights, after which she said goodnight to the two men and crawled into the shadow of the screen.

Yozo had a hard time falling asleep.

"It's cold," he said, shifting his position on the bed.

"Sure is," Kosuge said. "Sobered me up."

Mano cleared her throat. "Shall I get another blanket?"

Yozo squinted.

"Me? I'm fine. Can't sleep is all. It's the sound of the waves."

Kosuge took pity on Yozo. How perfectly mature of him. Needless to say, what Kosuge saw as pitiful was not actually Yozo, in his current situation, but the idea of himself in the same situation, or perhaps the situation as a general idea. Adults are thoroughly schooled in this way of seeing, which makes it quite easy for them to empathize with others. Each teardrop is a source of pride. Young people, it's true, will also sometimes indulge in this kind of trivial emotionality. But if adults acquire this ability only after making compromises with their lives, to put it generously, where do young people pick it up? From junk novels like this one?

"Hey, Mano, tell us a story. Know any good ones?"

Kosuge played the spoiled brat, taking it upon himself to brighten Yozo's mood.

"Hmmm," said Mano from the shadow of the screen. There was good humor in her voice, but she said no more.

"Don't hold back," said Kosuge. These boys were always itching for a thrill.

Mano must have been thinking it over, because she didn't respond right away.

"You can't tell anyone," she finally said, then added in a lower voice, "but it's a scary story. Will you be okay, Kosuge?"

"Sure, sure!" He was thrilled.

It happened the summer Mano was nineteen, at her first job as a nurse. A boy who had attempted suicide because of a woman was discovered and brought to the hospital. They asked Mano to take care of him. He had been using drugs. Purple dots up and down his body. It didn't look like they could save him.

That evening, however, he regained consciousness, one more time.

Outside the window, he saw a train of tiny shore crabs scuttling across the stone wall. They're so beautiful, he said. The crabs were alive, right as rain, but their shells were red, as if they'd been cooked. Once I'm better, I'll bring some of them home and make things right, he said, but then once more he lost consciousness.

That night, the patient filled the sink with vomit twice and died. Mano was tasked with waiting in the room with him until his family arrived. For about an hour, she did her best, sitting in a chair in the corner of the room, facing the wall. But then she thought she heard a sound behind her. Daring not to move a muscle, she heard the sound again, this time for certain. The pitter-pat of tiny feet. Bracing herself, she spun around, and just behind her on the floor was a little red crab. Seeing the creature, she began to cry.

"It was so strange. There really was a crab, right there. A real-life crab. I almost quit being a nurse, then and there. My family could survive just fine without me working anyway. But when I said so to my father, he just laughed at me – well, Kosuge, how was that?"

"Just grand," Kosuge shouted, hamming it up for her. "Which hospital was that?"

Hesitant to answer, Mano fidgeted around on her mat and spoke so quietly that they could barely hear her.

"When the hospital called me about Mr. Oba, I had half a mind to refuse. I was practically scared stiff. But once I showed up here and saw him, I was so relieved. He was already in such good shape and assured us from the start that he could use the lavatory on his own."

"I asked about the hospital, though. It wasn't this one, was it?"

It took Mano a second, but she answered.

"No, it was. This is the hospital. But like I said, you can't tell anyone I told you. My word is on the line."

Yozo spoke up in a sleepy voice. "Whoa, don't tell me it was this room."

"It wasn't."

"Whoa!" Kosuge said, parroting Yozo. "Don't tell me it was the room that we stayed in last night."

Mano laughed.

"It wasn't. Don't you worry. If I knew that it would bother you this much, why, I never would have told you."

"Room 6, then," said Kosuge, nodding wisely. "None of the other rooms have a view of the stone wall. It's gotta be Room 6. You realize that the patient staying there is just a girl? That's cruel."

"No reason to get excited. Let's go to bed. I was lying. I made the whole thing up."

But Yozo's thoughts were elsewhere. He was pondering the ghost of Sono. In his mind's eye, he could trace the gorgeous outline of her body. Yozo was capable, at times, of this kind of sincerity. To him and his friends, "god" was no more than a bit of chummy slang, something they said to express a mixture of derision and affection toward an idiotic person, but this was perhaps an indication of how close to god they actually were. I recognize that casually broaching the "question of a god," dear reader, may invite from you the criticism of me being superficial, or simplistic. Oh, please forgive me. Even the lowliest of authors has an urge to help his characters achieve a place closer to god than the rest of us. But I'll do you one better. Yozo was not merely close to god, but like one. Like the goddess of wisdom, Minerva, sending her sacred bird, the owl, out into the dusky sky and laughing to herself at the sight of it all.

The next day, the hospital came to life. It had snowed overnight. The thousand-some-odd dwarf pines growing in the front yard of the sanatorium were uniformly capped with snow, while all thirty of the steps down to the beach, and the sand for that matter, were covered with a modest dusting. The snow fell off and on until the middle of the day.

Yozo was in bed, lying on his belly as he sketched the snowy landscape. He'd sent Mano out to buy a pad of charcoal paper and a pencil but had only started working once the last of the snow had fallen.

The sanatorium was bright from the reflection of the snow. Kosuge lounged on the sofa, reading a magazine. Every once in a while he twisted his neck to see how Yozo's work was coming along. He felt a sense of reverence for the arts, however vague. It was a sentiment derived from his esteem for Yozo as a person. Kosuge had been watching him from a young age. He had always known that Yozo was a strange one. Playing with him throughout their childhood, he had come to the conclusion that this strangeness was a mark of his intelligence. Since they were boys, he had looked up to Yozo for his style and ability to lie, his eroticism and brutality. He was especially fond of the effulgent look that crept into his eyes during his student days, when he would gripe about his teachers. Yet unlike Hida, his fondness was that of a bystander. In that sense, he was tactful. He would stick with Yozo for as far as he could go, but once he found himself rolling his eyes, he took a step back and watched him from the sidelines. One might say that Kosuge was more modern than Yozo or Hida.

If there was anything of substance behind Kosuge's reverence for the arts, it was perfectly encapsulated by the anecdote above, where he visited the bathroom in his new blue overcoat. He tended to expect the best from life. In his view, if a man like Yozo put his blood, sweat, and tears into his work, the result would be nothing short of miraculous. It was a simple thing for him. Because he had the utmost confidence in Yozo. But on occasion, he was disappointed. Like now, for instance, stealing a glimpse of Yozo's sketch. He was repelled. The only thing drawn on the charcoal paper was a plain landscape of islands and sea. Normal sea and normal islands, too.

Kosuge gave up on the drawing and immersed himself in the story he'd been reading in the magazine. The room was a bit nippy.

Mano was elsewhere, washing Yozo's wool shirt in the laundry room. It was the shirt that he had worn into the ocean. Redolent with the aroma of the cliffs.

In the afternoon, Hida returned from the police station and barreled through the door.

"Wow!" he cried, seeing the sketch. "You've been working. That's fantastic. Artists are always better off when they're at work."

Hida walked over to the bed and glanced over Yozo's shoulder at the sheet of charcoal paper, but Yozo hurriedly folded the sheet in half and then again, into quarters.

"It's no use," he said in a bashful tone. "If I let it go too long, I wind up overthinking things."

Still wearing his overcoat, Hida sat down on the edge of the bed.

"I suppose so. Easy to get anxious. But there's nothing wrong with that at all. It's proof you're passionate about your art. At least, that's how I like to think of it – what were you drawing, anyway?"

Propping his face up with a palm, Yozo jutted his chin toward the view beyond the window glass.

"The sea. Sky and sea black, just the island white. But halfway through, it began to feel pretentious, so I stopped. The composition felt too amateurish to me."

"I think it's fine. All great artists are amateurs at heart. Nothing wrong with that at all. You start out as an amateur, work to become a pro, then become an amateur all over again. Just like Rodin. Now there was a man who embraced the genius of the amateur! Though I suppose that's open to debate."

Yozo stuffed the folded piece of charcoal paper in the sleeve of his kimono.

"I'm done with pictures," he said, as if to stifle Hida's train of thought. "They bore the living daylights out of me. And sculpture isn't any better."

Hida swept back his long hair and nodded in agreement. "I know the feeling."

"I think I'd prefer writing poetry. At least poems are honest."

"Sure, poems are great."

"But I'm afraid I'd be unsatisfied." He was prepared to be unsatisfied by absolutely anything. "What might suit me the best is to become a patron of the arts.

I'll make a bunch of money and use it all to dote upon a group of fine artists like you, Hida. How's that sound? I've had enough of making art myself."

Chin dug into his palm, Yozo looked out to sea, quietly awaiting a response.

"That doesn't sound half bad. I think it could be great for you. We need more people like that in the world. Sincerely." But as Hida said this, his voice faltered. He felt like a clown for being unable to refute any of this nonsense. But his pride, shall we say, as an artist had been so thoroughly bruised that he would have to speak. Hida braced himself. Oh, what to say!

"How'd things go with the police?" asked Kosuge, expecting the response to be wishy-washy.

Hida's perturbation found an outlet in this change of topic.

"They're charging him with aiding suicide," he said, then instantly regretted it. Much too blunt. "But I think there's a good chance that the case will be dismissed."

Kosuge, who had been sprawled out on the sofa, leapt to his feet and clapped his hands.

"You're in a pickle now!"

He had hoped to lighten the mood, but it was no use.

Yozo spun around and lay face up on the bed.

Surely by now, dear reader, you're disgusted with these young men for the carefree way in which they pass the time, as if one among them had not just killed another human being, though I suspect this new development will elicit shouts of joy. Serves him right, etc. How cruel of you. What part of what you see here is carefree? If only you could understand the sadness of the ones who grow the delicate flowers of buffoonery, protecting them from but the slightest gust of wind and always on the verge of despair!

Flustered by the unforeseen consequences of his comment, Hida patted Yozo's legs through the counterpane.

"It'll be okay. It'll be okay."

Kosuge fell back onto the sofa.

"Aiding suicide, huh?" he said, poking fun. "Is that even against the law?"

"Sure is," Yozo said, pulling his feet back. "Straight to the chain gang. And here I thought that you were studying law."

Hida smiled sadly.

"It's going to be okay. Your brother's taking care of everything. That's a strength of his. He's full of vigor."

"Gets things done." Kosuge solemnly closed his eyes. "Maybe there's no need to worry, after all. Your brother will finagle something."

"You jackass," Hida laughed.

He stood from the bed and slipped off his overcoat, which he hung on a hook beside the door.

"Here's some good news. About the woman's husband," he said, stepping over to a round Seto ware hibachi set by the doorway. After a moment's hesitation, he cast his eyes down and continued. "The husband met us at the station. He and your brother had a talk, the two of them, you see. When your brother told me what the guy told him, I was shocked. He said he didn't want a cent, just wanted to meet the boyfriend. Your brother told him no. That you were in the hospital and all distraught about what happened. So the guy gave him this miserable look and said to tell his little brother that he sends his best regards, that there's no hard feelings between the two of you, to get well soon – " but Hida stopped himself.

He was worked up; his choice of language was too potent for his own good. This was a glorified version of the story, skewed by Hida's repressed indignation toward Yozo's brother, which had been stoked by the cruel way he'd smirked when he mentioned that the husband had been dressed in rags, like someone on the dole.

"He should have let him visit me. Who's he think he is, the director?" Yozo stared into the palm of his right hand.

A shiver passed through Hida's copious physique.

"Right – but I think he made the right call. It's best the two of you remain strangers. He already went back to Tokyo, anyhow. Your brother saw him off at the station. Gave him two hundred yen as a sign of his condolences. He even had him sign a letter saying that you have no further obligation to him or his kin."

"Gets things done all right." Kosuge nodded, sticking out his skinny bottom lip. "Just two hundred yen? What a deal."

Hida grimaced painfully, his rotund face starting to shine in the warm glow of the hibachi. These boys were haunted by a fear of having cold water thrown on them in the middle of a good time. Hence their pattern of enabling each other. They did their best to match each other's moods. It was an unspoken condition of their friendship. Kosuge was violating their agreement, perhaps, but he couldn't understand why Hida was so deeply moved by what amounted to another piece of gossip. He found the weakness of the husband irritating, but was unsurprised that Yozo's brother saw it as an opportunity.

Hida shuffled around Yozo's bed and over to the windows. Pressing his nose against the glass, he gazed out upon the waves, beneath the cloudy sky.

"I think that husband is a classy guy. This isn't about whether his brother gets things done or not. That's not what happened. That guy's got class. Something beautiful happens when a human being surrenders. They cremated her this morning, you know. The guy went back to Tokyo carrying the ashes in the urn. I can still see him, leaning from the window of the train."

Kosuge finally got the picture. He let out a deep sigh. "A moving tale."

"Isn't it, though? I think it's grand." Hida spun his head around to see Kosuge. The mood had been saved after all. "Hearing this kind of story makes me glad to be alive."

Excuse me, but I have to intervene. Otherwise I won't be able to continue. This novel is a total mess. I'm making myself dizzy. Yozo is too much for me, and Kosuge is too much for me, and Hida is too much for me as well. They grow impatient with my clumsy style and zip away like so much quicksilver. I swat my hands at their muddy shoes and shout for them to wait, please wait. Unless I whip my boys here into shape, I don't think I can take this anymore.

This novel was doomed from the start. All posture and no substance. Whether I write one page or a hundred, it amounts to the same thing. Though I knew this from the start. Call me optimistic. I assumed that in the course of writing, I would stumble upon some redeeming quality. I'm a hack, it's true. But who says that a hack job can't have some redeeming quality? Even as I tired of my overzealous, tacky prose, I searched high and low for some small part worth saving. Yet over time, the passions of my heart grew cold. And now I'm pooped. Alas, a novel must be written from a place of innocence! What's that you say? Beautiful feelings make bad literature? Bullshit. Never have I heard so treacherous a phrase. Without transcendence, who could write a novel to completion? Every word and every sentence would assail the heart with a dozen possible meanings, until you had no choice but to snap your pen in half and toss it in the trash.

What business does Yozo or Hida or Kosuge have behaving so outrageously? They'll only give themselves away.

Easy now, easy now. Take a breath and clear your mind.

る

That evening, quite late in fact, Yozo's brother visited his room. Yozo was playing card games with Hida and Kosuge. Come to think of it, they had been playing cards the day before as well, when his brother came the first time. But this is not to say these young men played cards all day, every day. No sir. On the contrary, they'd just as soon never play at all; they only broke the deck out when they were so bored they could cry. Card games were their last resort, but even so, they shied away from any game that didn't afford them full expression of their personalities. Card tricks were their preference. They messed around, creating their own versions of all kinds of different card tricks, showing off. All too proud to give away their secrets. Cracking up.

But they took it one step further. One of them would lay a card face down on the table and have the others guess. Queen of spades? Jack of clubs? Each player thinks it over, really hard, then takes a wild guess. The card is flipped – never have they ever guessed it right, but someday they probably will, or so they think. What pleasure it would be to find yourself the lucky dog!

Suffice to say, these boys did not go in for lengthy competitions. They liked high stakes. All or nothing. Games decided in a flash. Which is why the cards were never out for more than ten minutes or so. A mere ten-minute window, once a day. And somehow, Yozo's brother had arrived during that tiny window twice.

This time, he frowned at what he saw. Mistakenly assuming that these boys did nothing else. Cards all the livelong day. This sort of mishap is a fact of life, though. Yozo had a mishap much like this one back in art school. During one of his French lessons, he let a yawn slip out three different times, making eye contact with the professor on all three occasions. The old professor, one of the foremost scholars of the French language in all of Japan, lost his patience around yawn number three and gave Yozo a piece of his mind. "Why must you waste my time with all these yawns? A hundred in the past hour alone." The way he said it, you would think that he had counted all those yawns on his ten fingers ten times over.

See what happens when I take a breath and clear my mind? Leave me alone for two seconds and I'm rambling on and on again. Now I really need to whip my boys into shape. Writing from a place of innocence is more than I can hope for. Where on earth is this book going? Let's take another look and recap from the beginning.

I'm writing a novel about a sanatorium, set on the coast. The view of the ocean is apparently quite nice. And the people at the sanatorium are nice, too. Not one bad egg among them. Which is especially true of these three young men, who, I'll just say it, they're my heroes. That's it. Who needs a complicated pretext? Not me. I'm only here to advocate for these three men. All right, here we go. Here goes nothing. Don't talk back.

Yozo's brother said a quick hello to everyone, then whispered something into Hida's ear. Hida nodded and glanced at Kosuge and Mano.

His brother waited for the other three to leave before addressing Yozo.

"Dim lights in here."

"Yeah, they don't allow bright lights in the hospital," said Yozo, sitting on the sofa. "Care to sit?"

"Sure." But instead of sitting down, his brother paced the tiny room, frequently looking up at the dim lights that had stolen his attention. "I've more or less straightened things out for you."

"Thanks," said Yozo quietly, bowing his head.

"I could care less about what happened, but next time you go home, you're gonna get an earful." Today he had not shown up in a hakama. Inexplicably, his black haori was missing the strings that close the front. "I'll do whatever I can do to help, but if I were you, I'd sit down and write Dad a proper letter. You guys seem like you're having a great time, but I'll have you know, this is no laughing matter."

Yozo had nothing to say. He picked up one of the playing cards spread across the sofa and gave it a long, hard look.

"If you can't bring yourself to do that, fine. The day after tomorrow, you and I are going to the station. They've been kind enough to forgo questioning you this long. Today they questioned me and Hida, as official witnesses. They asked me how you normally behaved, so I told them you were on the quiet side. They also asked if I had any doubts as to your mental health, but I said absolutely not."

He stopped walking around the room and paused by the hibachi on the floor near Yozo, where he held his big hands to the incandescent coals. Yozo watched his brother's hands in a daze, noticing them twitch ever so slightly.

"They asked about the woman, too. I said I didn't know a thing about her. Seems like they questioned Hida about mostly the same things. And thankfully, it matched up with my testimony. I expect the same from you. Stick to the facts."

Yozo understood what his brother was trying to say, but he feigned ignorance.

"The facts?"

"Don't tell them any more than necessary. Just answer all the questions clearly, whatever they ask."

"I wonder if they'll prosecute," said Yozo, tracing the edge of the card with his pointer finger.

"Hard to say. That's hard to say," his brother told him, more emphatically than before. "I suspect they'll lock you up for four or five days, anyway, so you may as well get ready. I'll come back for you the morning after next. We'll head down there together."

His brother watched the embers, quiet for a time. The sound of trickling snow mixed with the action of the waves.

"The particulars of these events aside," he began awkwardly, then switched over to a more deliberately informal tone. "It's about time you thought about where your life is heading, down the road. There isn't nearly as much family money as you think. This year's harvest was a bust. I'm not expecting you to care, but our local bank has fallen on hard times. It's pandemonium. Don't laugh, but whether you're an artist or a normal person like the rest of us, you have to worry about keeping food on the table. But you're in a good place. You have a second chance. You might try breaking a sweat for a change. Well, it's getting late. I think it'd be best for you if Hida and Kosuge spent the night with me. If you guys keep causing a ruckus every night, it'll be hell to pay."

"I've got some pretty good friends, huh?"

Yozo was in bed, facing away from Mano. She had moved back to her usual quarters on the sofa for the night.

"I agree – especially Kosuge." She carefully adjusted her position. "I find him very entertaining."

"Yeah. I mean, he's still a kid. Three years younger than me, so, twenty-two? Same as my dead little brother. All of my bad habits have been rubbing off on him. Hida, though, he's a different story. That guy's got it figured out. Under control." He paused for a moment, then continued in a lower voice. "Every time I get into a mess like this, he does everything he can to console me. He'd

71

rather laugh with us than call us out. He's a strong guy, at least in most other respects, but when it comes to standing up to us, he's as timid as they come. Won't do."

Mano was quiet.

"Want to hear about this woman?"

From the sluggish way he said it, turned away from her, you'd think it was the last thing that he wanted to discuss. When he felt the least bit awkward, Yozo had no idea how to skirt the situation. Instead, he had a sorry habit of doubling down on the awkwardness.

"It's not much of a story," he began, since Mano hadn't responded. "You must have heard by now, but her name was Sono. She worked at a bar in Ginza. I probably only went three times, maybe four. Not enough for Hida or Kosuge to find out. And I never told them." Had enough yet? "Not much of a story. She wanted to kill herself because living was too much for her. Up until the very end, our heads were in completely different places. Just before we jumped into the water, Sono had to go and tell me, 'You look just like my old man, the schoolteacher.' She had a common-law husband. I guess he taught elementary school until a few years ago. What was I thinking, trying to end my life with a person like her? I must have really loved her after all."

The man can no longer be trusted. How can these guys be so bad at telling stories about themselves?

"All the while, I was working for the left. Handing out leaflets, staging demonstrations, all kinds of things I wasn't cut out to do. It was absurd. But it was tough work. What kept me going was this fantasy of being some kind of an enlightened person. That only got me so far, though. No matter how I struggled, things always fell apart. There's a good chance that I'll wind up on the streets, a beggar. If the family business goes bankrupt, I won't know where to turn to for my next meal. I don't have any skills or trades. Hell, I'm more or less a beggar already."

The more he spoke, the more he sounded to himself like a scoundrel. Such was his misfortune!

"I believe in destiny. Not forcing things. What I really want to do is paint. Like you wouldn't believe." Yozo scratched his head and laughed. "To paint something good for once."

To paint something good for once, he said. And said it laughing. Young people never say anything straight. You can tell they're being honest if they hide behind a laugh.

The day dawned. Not a wisp of cloud in the sky. Yesterday's snow had disappeared, except for a few discolored patches in the shadows of the pines or in the crannies of the stone steps. Mist billowed off the sea, an endless mist through which the engines of the fishing boats could be heard piloting the waters.

The director checked on Yozo first thing in the morning. After giving him a thorough physical examination, he blinked his beady eyes behind his spectacles and offered an opinion.

"Overall, I'd say you're in good shape. Just take it easy. I'll be sure to apprise the police as to your present circumstances. You don't quite have your strength back, not yet. Well then, Mano, you can take the dressing off his face now."

Mano peeled away the gauze. His wounds had healed. The scab had come off with the bandages, revealing pale but pinkly mottled skin.

"Please don't take this the wrong way, but I hope you've learned your lesson."

The director looked away, almost bashful, turning his eyes toward the sea.

Yozo felt uncomfortable as well. Without standing from the bed, he redid his kimono and said nothing in response.

Just then, the door flew open with a wave of screeching laughter, as Hida and Kosuge barged into the room. Everybody said good morning. The director told the two guests they were looking well, but then his voice grew melancholy.

"Last full day with us. We'll be sad to see you go."

With that, the director took his leave. Kosuge was the first to open his mouth.

"A proper gentleman. With the mug of an octopus."

These guys were fascinated with the human face, prepared to judge a person's total worth based purely on the arrangement of their facial features.

"There's a picture of him in the cafeteria," Kosuge said. "Wearing his medals."

"Lousy painting," Hida said over his shoulder as he stepped onto the balcony.

Today, he was dressed in a kimono that he'd borrowed from Yozo's brother. The fabric was brown and thick. He sat down on the rattan balcony chair, making sure the neck of the kimono wasn't twisted.

"From this angle, Hida, I might mistake you for a maestro after all."

Kosuge joined him on the balcony.

"Hey Yozo, wanna play cards?"

They pulled the chair outside and began a game that had no rhyme or reason.

Partway through, Kosuge spoke up in a serious tone.

"What's with the pose, Hida?"

"You're the one posing, idiot. Look at your hands!"

The three young men burst out laughing, but all at once they snuck a look at the other balconies down the wing. The patients from Rooms 5 and 6 were out too, sunbathing on their daybeds, and laughing so hard at what the guys were up to they were red in the face.

"Oh no! We've been caught!"

Kosuge dropped his jaw and turned to Yozo. The three of them roared with laughter, really screaming now. These boys were known to play the buffoon. If Kosuge broke out the deck of cards, Hida and Yozo took the cue and ran with it. They knew the choreography by heart, down to the final curtain.

Whenever they found themselves in a beautiful natural setting, they couldn't help but stage a performance. Perhaps it was a way to commemorate the moment. In this case, the backdrop for their stage was the morning sea. But their cries of laughter brought about a major incident not one of them could have expected.

You see, Mano was accosted by the sanatorium's head nurse, her boss. Within five minutes of the hullabaloo erupting from the balconies, she was summoned to her office, harshly reprimanded, and sent away to shut them up. Mano flew out of the office crying. By the time she reached the three friends and informed them about what had happened, they had finished playing cards and were lounging around the room.

The boys were thoroughly deflated by the news; all that they could do was glance at one another. Their ecstatic comedy had been knocked flat by the voice of reason, which ordered them to cut it out and laughed at them, not with them, spoiling the fun. It was a nearly fatal blow.

"You're not bothering anyone," said Mano, as if it was her job to console them. "None of the patients in this wing are in critical condition. And get this: last night, I ran into the mother of the girl who's in Room 5, in the hallway, who told me she appreciated how friendly things have been here. She said she and her daughter have been laughing every day, at all the funny things her neighbors have been saying. Everything's fine. Not to worry."

"No. It isn't fine," said Kosuge, standing from the sofa. "Because of us, you had to take a scolding. Why can't she come down here and tell us to our faces? I say you bring her down here. If she hates having us here that much, she should just kick us out. We'd gladly leave at any time."

In a split second, the three friends had made up their minds. They were getting out of here. Most of all Yozo, who was already imagining the four of them together in a speeding automobile, making a glorious escape up the coast.

Hida stood up from the sofa too. He was smiling.

"How about it? Let's go down there ourselves and give the head nurse a piece of our minds. We'll show her for yelling at us!"

"Let's get out of here," said Kosuge. He nudged the door with his toe. "Who wants to sit around a lousy hospital? I could care less about getting yelled at. What bugs me is how they treated us up until now. They seem to think we're just a bunch of little shits, idiotic bourgeois poseurs with no personalities, born yesterday."

When he was done, Kosuge kicked the door again, this time a little harder. But then he cracked up laughing, unable to contain himself.

Yozo flopped down on the bed so hard the springs creaked. "If you're a little shit, I suppose that makes me a pale-skinned romantic. Can't have that."

Their blood boiled in the wake of this barbaric effrontery, but after a sad moment of reflection, they shook it off as if it were a joke. That was their style.

Mano, however, was direct. Both arms clasped behind her back, she leaned against the wall by the door and stuck out her curled upper lip, so that it curled up even further.

"You're exactly right. They treated you like garbage. Meanwhile, no one seems to care that last night all of the nurses had a grand old time down at the office playing karuta."

"Exactly," Yozo said. "I could hear them screaming well past midnight. Pretty stupid, if you ask me."

Yozo grabbed one of the sheets of charcoal paper strewn across the bed and started doodling, reclined.

"That head nurse is up to no good, so she's unable to see the good in others. I hear she spends her nights with the director."

"Oh really! I'm starting to like her." Kosuge was enthused. These boys thought of scandal as a virtue.

There was hope for the old nurse yet. "Well then, Mr. Medals has a mistress, huh? I'm starting to like these two."

"But really, none of you has done anything wrong. You're just having a good time. Some harmless jokes, a couple laughs. Why can't she understand? You should just ignore her altogether. Have as much fun as you like. Doesn't bother me at all. This is your last full day here. To think, nice men like you, from decent families, who've never been in trouble once, in your whole lives . . ."

Mano pressed a hand to her cheek. Just like that, she was crying her eyes out. Crying as she pushed open the door.

Hida tried to stop her. "Don't go down there. Hold on. It's not worth it."

Covering her face with her hands, she nodded repeatedly and went out into the hall.

"A champion of justice," said Kosuge, once Mano was gone. He smirked and sat down on the sofa. "Those were some real tears. I think that speech of hers went to her head. She may talk like a grownup, all professional, but hey, she is a woman after all."

"She's strange all right." Hida walked up and down the tiny room. "I always knew that there was something strange about her. There's something going on. She scared me when she started crying and went flying for the door. I could've sworn that she was going straight to the head nurse."

"She'd never do that," Yozo said, putting on a cool expression, then whipped the charcoal paper doodle at Kosuge.

"Wow, is this a portrait of the head nurse?"

Kosuge laughed so hard he practically collapsed.

"What now?" Hida glanced at the sheet of charcoal paper. "A monster of a woman. Masterful. Is that really what she looks like?"

"Spitting image," said Kosuge. "She came down here once, you know, with the director. Excellent work. Hey, gimme that."

Kosuge took the pencil from Yozo and added something to the illustration.

"There you go, a nice new pair of horns. Now it really looks like her. Let's stick it to her office door, huh?"

"Come on, time for a stroll."

Yozo got out of bed and stretched. And while he stretched, he gave himself a little compliment.

"A stroll with the master of caricature."

か

Master of caricature! I think I'm finally losing patience
with myself. Is this a dime novel or what? I had hoped for
this scene to serve as something of an antidote for my
tense nerves, and for yours, too, dear reader, but that last
bit was way too cheesy. If this book does become a classic
– goodness, have I lost my mind? Surely these asides are
doing you more harm than good. You don't need me. You
can draw your own conclusions, things the author never
could imagine. Then you'll tell it from the mountain why
this novel is a classic, crying out for all to hear.

Boy, do the dead masters have it good. Meanwhile,
the hacks up here among the living waste themselves
away, burying their work in misguided commentary, in

the hopes that it might win the admiration of even one more reader. The result is an abomination, laden with ridiculously tedious asides. Alas, I lack the fortitude to throw a pie in my own face and bellow, "Pull yourself together, man!"

I guess I'll never be a great writer. I'm a softy. I'll admit it. At least we've figured that much out. A softy through and through. But in my softness I find peace, however fleeting. Ah, it doesn't matter anymore. Forget I said anything. It would seem the flowers of buffoonery have shriveled up at last. And shriveled up into a mean, disgusting, dirty mess while they were at it.

The desire for perfection. The lure of the master-piece.

Oh, Creator of Miracles, I've had enough! Why me?

Mano was holed up in the bathroom. Ready to cry her heart out. But she didn't cry for long. Gazing into the mirror, she wiped away her tears, fixed her hair, and made her way down to the cafeteria for a late breakfast.

At a table by the entrance, the college student from Room 1 sat before an empty bowl of soup, looking bored as can be.

The sight of Mano made him smile.

"Seems like the new guy's doing well."

Mano stood there with him for a moment, gripping a corner of the table.

"Sure is. One harmless joke after another, making us all laugh."

"Gee, that's swell. He's an artist, huh?"

"That's right. He's always saying how he wants to paint something extraordinary." This made Mano blush from ear to ear. "He's serious. But being serious, or serious like that, can put you through a world of pain."

"Too true. Too true."

The student blushed, wholeheartedly agreeing. The fact that he'd received permission to go home soon had lifted him to a new height of generosity.

What a sentimental gal. Say reader, what's not to love about a woman like her? Bah! I know, I know, I must sound hopelessly old-fashioned. Go on then, laugh. At this point, even fleeting peace is too much for me to bear. I cannot love a woman without smothering her with commentary. Proof that if a man is dumb enough, he can do harm without lifting a finger.

"That's it, that spot over there."

Yozo pointed at a big, flat cliff that could be seen through the branches of a pear tree. Here and there, yesterday's snow clung to divots in the rocks.

"That's where we jumped," he said, eyes opened wide, as if this were a punchline.

Kosuge was quiet. He couldn't help but wonder about what was going on in Yozo's heart, behind his even-keeled delivery. Which isn't to say that Yozo sounded neutral, just that he knew how to say this sort of thing without flinching.

"Shall we head back?" asked Hida, pinching his kimono with both hands to keep the hem off the sand.

The three of them reversed course and walked back up the beach. The sea was calm. In the noonday sun, it was a sheet of white.

Yozo tossed a stone into the water.

"It felt great. I knew the second that I jumped, all of my problems would be gone. No more worries about debts, or the academy, or family, or regrets, or my masterpiece, or shame, or Marxism, or even about any of my friends, or trees or flowers. Suddenly, I'm standing on that cliff and laughing. It felt great."

Kosuge gathered shells to hide his agitation.

Hida forced a laugh.

"Don't make it sound too good. It's giving me the creeps."

Yozo laughed too. Their footsteps in the sand made a pleasant crunching sound.

"Don't get upset. I was exaggerating." Yozo touched shoulders with Hida as they walked. "But here's a bit of truth. Want to know what she whispered to me just before we jumped?"

Kosuge narrowed his eyes. They burned with morbid curiosity. He kept his distance from the other two.

"I can hear it now. *I miss the way we talked back home*, she said. She grew up in a place way south of here, you see."

"Stop. That's too much!"

"It's true, though. Truly. Hah. Par for the course with her."

A large fishing boat had been pulled up onto the sand. Beside it rested two magnificent fish baskets, each nearly eight feet across. Kosuge took aim at the boat's black hull and chucked all the shells he had collected in a single toss.

They were silent for a time. The three boys felt so awkward that they nearly suffocated. In another minute, they might have all thrown themselves into the sea.

But then Kosuge broke the seal.

"Look, look!" he shouted, pointing down the beach. "It's Room 5 and Room 6!"

The two young ladies were coming down the beach spinning white parasols, odd for December.

"Bingo!" Yozo had come back to life.

"Care to say hello?" Kosuge lifted up one of his shoes to brush the sand away, then looked at Yozo, waiting for the signal. Ready to lunge forth as soon as he said the word.

"Easy, now."

Hida gave Kosuge a stern look and grabbed his shoulder.

The parasols wobbled to a halt. The girls appeared to be talking something over, but soon enough they spun around and briskly started off.

"We can catch up with them." Now Yozo was the one getting excited, but then he saw Hida's frowning face. "Never mind."

Hida was hopelessly forlorn. In that instant, he felt his lukewarm temperament all too keenly, the forces pulling him away from his two friends. He wondered if a difference in their lifestyles was to blame, for Hida was comparatively poor.

"A good sign, if you ask me." Kosuge shrugged like a Hollywood dandy. He was trying to do whatever he could to recover the situation. "They saw us out here walking and came down to have a look. Just a couple of kids. Poor things. They're all mixed up. See, now they're picking up shells. Like a couple of copycats."

Hida couldn't help but grin, but he caught Yozo looking back at him with sorrow in his eyes. They blushed, in spite of themselves. They had an understanding. A desire to console each other filled their hearts. They were suckers for fragility.

Feeling the faint warmth of the ocean breeze, the three boys walked back up the beach, watching the far-off parasols.

At the foot of the white sanatorium, even farther down the shore, Mano stood and waited for them to return. She raised her right hand to her forehead as a visor, blocking out the glare.

On the last night, Mano was ebullient. Well after they'd gone to bed, she chattered on and on about her humble upbringing and her noble lineage. As the night progressed, Yozo grew unresponsive. He turned away from her and offered vague responses, as his thoughts were elsewhere.

At one point, Mano finally shared the story of the scar above her eye.

"Okay, when I was three ..." She started off nonchalantly, but she faltered and her voice cracked. "So, I flipped over a lamp and burned myself. It made me horribly self-conscious for the longest time. When I went off to elementary school, the scar felt so, so big on my face. My friends at school called me Hotaru. Hotaru . . ."

Firefly. She trailed off for a moment.

"That was my nickname. Except every time they said it, I felt this crazy need to take revenge. I really mean it, too. I wanted power."

She laughed to herself.

"Pretty silly. Power over what? Maybe I should just wear glasses. If I wore glasses, then I bet the scar would be a bit harder to see."

"Come on! That would only make it worse," Yozo blurted out, as if personally offended. When he felt love for a woman, he had a funny way of showing it – old-fashioned even then – by being cruel. "It's fine the way it is. Barely noticeable. Come on, let's get some sleep. It's gonna be an early morning."

Mano was quiet. *Tomorrow we'll say goodbye*, she thought. *But I barely even know him. Shame on me, shame on me. Where's my sense of dignity?* She coughed and sighed and whacked the mattress left and right, tossing and turning violently.

Yozo pretended not to notice. Whatever he had on his mind, I cannot say.

Instead, I'll ask you now to lend your ears to the sounds of the waves and the voices of the gulls, as we look back on the events of the past four days. The stubborn realist might describe these days as one big farce. But the real farce is the fact that this manuscript spent the majority of its time on submission serving as a coaster for my editor's teapot and was mailed back to me with a big black ring burned into the top page. The real farce is the way I blame my wife's dark past for my troubles, as I swing from joy to sorrow. The real farce is in the way I straighten my collar as I duck into the pawnshop, thinking that swagger will conceal how far I've fallen. We're all a bunch of clowns. If you want to see a farce, look in the mirror.

A man crushed by reality puts on a show of endurance. If that's beyond your comprehension, dear reader, then you and I will never understand each other. Life's a farce, so we might as well make it a good one. But real life is a realm that I may never reach. The best that I can hope for is to loiter in the memory of these four days, so steeped with empathy. Four days that count more than five or ten years of my life. Four days that count more than a lifetime.

He could hear Mano gently breathing. She was asleep. Yozo was unable to contain his excitement. He turned to face her, wriggling his lanky body with delight, but just then a raspy voice whispered in his ear:

Stop! You mustn't betray Hotaru's trust.

At the first sign of night's transition into morning, the two of them were already awake. Today was the day Yozo would be discharged from the hospital. I'd been dreading the arrival of this day ... with the disgusting fondness of a hack. My hope was that by writing this novel, I could somehow rescue Yozo. Or rather, I'd hoped the novel would redeem yours truly, a slimy fox who's failed to live up to his Byronic ideals. This was my secret prayer, kept hidden in my suffering. But as that fateful day approached, I felt a sense of desolation, so much stronger than before, returning to haunt Yozo and myself. This novel is a failure. It has no climax, no denouement. It seems I paid too much attention to the style. As a result, the story is a heap of purple trash. I bogged it down with lots of things nobody needs to hear. But I also left out lots of vital details. Not to be pompous, but if I live a long life and look back over these pages at some point in the future, I'm sure to be repulsed by what I find. Before I can get through a single page, I'll shudder with unbearable self-loathing and shut the book. Even now, I barely have the strength to reread what I've written. Ah, a writer must never reveal themselves like this. That's his undoing. Beautiful feelings, that's how we make bad literature. I've used this phrase three times now. And you know what? I stand behind it.

I don't know the first thing about literature. Perhaps I should start fresh, from the beginning. But where, dear reader, should I begin?

What am I but a tangle of uncertainty and pride? That just about sums up this novel. Ah, why do I hasten to pass judgment on everything? Who instilled me with this sick imperative to pin down every thought?

Shall I write the rest? The last scene at Blue Pines. It can only go one way.

Mano proposed they climb the hill, to see the view.

"It's so delightful. If we hurry, we'll be able to see Fuji."

Yozo kept his neck warm with a woolen muffler, black as can be. Mano, over her nurse's uniform, wore a haori with a pattern like pine needles, then wrapped herself in a red shawl several times, nearly burying her face.

They stepped into their geta and clopped off into the field behind the sanatorium. On the north side of the grounds was a cliff of red clay, outfitted with a narrow metal ladder. Mano opted to go first, darting nimbly up the rungs.

They found the hillside covered with dry grass laden with frost.

Mano blew on her fingertips to warm them up and continued up the trail, practically running. They could see their breath. The trail had a gradual incline with many twists and turns. Yozo trampled through the frost, trying to keep up. He whistled a jaunty tune into the frozen air. They had the whole hill to themselves. They could do anything they wanted. A whistle brightened up the mood. He would hate for Mano to get the wrong idea.

The trail dipped into a gully. This too was covered with dry sedge grass. Mano paused there for a moment. Yozo stopped five or six steps behind her. Just off the trail was a white tentlike structure.

Mano pointed at the tent.

"This is a sunbathing station. Patients with minor symptoms are welcome to come up here and sunbathe in the nude. Even now."

Frost sparkled on the canvas of the tent.

"Let's keep going," Yozo said.

For some reason, he felt anxious.

Mano started off again. Yozo followed her. They came upon a tunnel of skinny larch trees. Both of them were tired, so they slowed down to a leisurely stroll.

Shoulders heaving as he breathed, Yozo spoke to Mano in a booming outdoor voice.

"Hey, are you stuck down here for New Year's?"

Without turning around, she responded just as loudly.

"No, I think I'm heading back to Tokyo!"

"In that case, come by and say hello. Hida and Kosuge come over almost every day. Doesn't seem like I'll be ringing in the new year from a jail cell. Things are going to work out fine, I'm sure of it."

In his mind's eye, the enigmatic prosecutor turned to him and winked.

Shall I end there? The old masters always end things on a high note, something rich with meaning. But this flimsy brand of solace has gotten rather old for me, and for Yozo, and for you as well, I bet, dear reader. Who cares about New Year's or the prosecutor? Did the question of the prosecutor even cross your mind? All of us just want to make it to the summit. What's up there? What could it be? Our one remaining source of hope, however illusory.

At last, they made it to the top. The summit had been leveled off, making a clearing of red earth. In the middle of it was a low-slung picnic shelter, logs for posts, complete with flagstones and the like. Frost dusted everything.

"Darn. We can't see Fuji after all!" Mano shouted, the tip of her nose pink from the cold. "It's usually such a perfect view from here."

She pointed to the cloudy skies in the east. The morning sun had yet to show itself. Scud clouds of the strangest colors climbed and burst only to settle, though not settling for long before they drifted into nothing.

"Nah, it's fine."

A slight breeze cut across their cheeks.

Yozo looked out over the ocean, far below. He was only a few steps from a three-hundred-foot drop, below which Enoshima was a little bump just off the shore. Under the heavy morning mists, the seawater was churning.

And then – no, that's all I have.